Watch Out For Willie!

Willie dangled one leg through the ladder as she worked on the top of the mural. The ladder creaked and shook.

"Be careful," said Emily.

"Don't worry," said Willie. The ladder swayed to the right. "It's not going to break." She bent even farther. The ladder tilted onto three legs. "Uh-oh!"

The next thing Missy saw was Willie being hurled through the air. "Help!" she yelled.

Like a shot being fired from a cannon, Willie flew across the room, landing squarely on top of Missy's new canopy. *R-r-r-rip,* went the fabric as Willie tore through the roof and fell with a plop into the middle of Missy's bed.

THE ROOM OF DOOM

by Molly Albright

illustrated by Eulala Conner

Troll Associates

Library of Congress Cataloging-in-Publication Data

Albright, Molly.
  The room of doom / by Molly Albright; illustrated by Eulala
Conner.
    p.   cm.
  Summary: Chaos erupts when twelve-year-old Missy has all her
friends help her redecorate her room at the same time a famous
designer is "doing" her neighbor Stephanie's house.
  ISBN 0-8167-1482-7 (lib. bdg.)   ISBN 0-8167-1483-5 (pbk.)
  [1. Interior decoration—Fiction.] I. Conner, Eulala, ill.
II. Title.
PZ7.A325Ro 1989
[Fic]—dc19   88-15912

A TROLL BOOK, published by Troll Associates,
Mahwah, NJ 07430

Printed in the United States of America.

10 9 8 7 6 5 4 3 2 1

THE ROOM OF DOOM

CHAPTER

1

——

"Missy, clean your room!"

Twelve-year-old Melissa Fremont looked up from the magazine she was reading with an innocent expression on her face. "Who, me?"

Missy's mother stuck her head inside the doorway and frowned. "You heard me, young lady. This room is a disaster!"

Missy slowly glanced around. The pile of clothes on her desk chair was so huge that no one could see the chair. Dirty dishes and an empty cookie carton littered the floor. She hadn't made her bed or changed her sheets in weeks. "Maybe things *are* a little out of control," Missy thought, "but it isn't my fault."

"Mom, where am I supposed to put all this stuff?" she said. "There's no room in my closet anymore. Everything's spilling over."

"I noticed," said her mother. She grinned and

nodded toward the pile of clothes on the chair. "Are those clean or dirty?"

"I'm not sure," said Missy. She smiled brightly. "If I had one of those closet organizers, it'd be a lot easier to clean up. What do you think?"

"Hmmm," said her mother. "This sounds like a plot."

"And look at my dresser," Missy continued. "I've had it since I was a baby. It still has purple crayon marks on it, and it's all chipped and crummy." She held up the magazine she was reading. "It says here in *The Complete Decorator* that 'redecorating needn't be costly. All it takes is a little time and imagination.'"

Pat Fremont laughed. "Aha! The plot thickens!"

"Mom," said Missy. "I'm serious. Nobody has sheets with bears on them anymore. Don't you agree that this room needs help?"

Missy's mother nodded. "Absolutely," she said. "It needs to be cleaned."

Missy sighed. Ever since they'd moved to Indianapolis from Cincinnati, Missy had been wanting to redecorate her room. Her mother smiled at her. "I'll tell you what," she said, "you clean up this room and maybe we can talk about redecorating."

Missy's face brightened. "Really?"

"Really," said her mother. "I'll talk to your dad about it when he gets home." Missy's father played first viola in the Indianapolis Symphony. Missy's mother playfully shook her finger. "Now get to work, young lady. Next time I come in here I want to be able to walk from the door to the bed without having to clear a path."

Missy watched her mother disappear down the hall. Then she hopped off her bed. "Calling Baby Fremont," she bellowed. "Room service, please."

Seconds later Missy's Old English sheepdog bounded through the door. Baby was Missy's best friend and like Missy, he had been adopted when he was only a few weeks old. Missy and Baby were two of a kind—they did everything together!

"Guess what?" Missy announced. "Mom says if I clean my room, she'll talk to Dad about redecorating. Isn't that great?"

Baby wagged his tail and barked.

"Want to help?" she said.

Baby flattened his ears.

"Please?" said Missy. "I promise it won't take long." She cleared a space for them both at the foot of the bed and together they sifted through the mess. There were comic books, one pink knee sock, a button from a winter coat, a hairbrush, an old doll named Darlene. "Wow! Here's my Cincinnati Reds pennant!" Missy said, pulling it out from underneath a checkers game.

She held up the pennant and grinned. "Remember when Grandma took us to that game?" she said. "We both ate so many hot dogs we threw up on the way home."

Baby barked and wagged his tail.

All this work was starting to get exhausting. Missy leaned back against the bed and sighed.

Then she saw Baby's Frisbee, peeking out from the foot of the bed. "Here, Baby, catch!"

The Frisbee sailed across the room.

Baby leapt up, knocking over all the piles Missy had just made. "Good catch!" she said as Baby's jaws snapped around the Frisbee. He trotted over to the bed and dropped it into her lap. "Here comes a pop fly," she said, tossing it high into the air again.

This time Baby shot straight up, narrowly missing the light fixture. He caught the Frisbee in mid-air. "Bravo!" said Missy.

Baby crashed to the floor. "Watch out for the wastebasket," Missy said, but it was too late. The wastebasket toppled across the floor, spilling its contents onto Missy's white carpet. "Uh-oh," said Missy when she saw some cherry soda spill out of a can. She quickly tried to blot the stain with a comic book.

"Missy, what's going on in there?" called her mother, right on cue.

"Nothing, Mom," she said. She threw the comic book over the stain.

Mrs. Fremont appeared in the doorway. "What happened in here?" she gasped. "It looks like a tornado just hit!"

"We've just been cleaning up," Missy said. "Can't you see the piles?" She pointed to a vague spot on the floor.

"Hmmm," said her mother.

"We've been working really hard," said Missy, edging her way toward the door. "Right, Baby?"

Baby barked.

"And now we're going to the park to play a little Frisbee. We need a break."

"But what about your room?" said her mother.

Missy looked at the mess once more. "Don't worry, Mom," she said in her most hopeful voice. "We'll finish it later."

That evening during dinner Missy brought up the subject of redecorating again. "Mom, this casserole is delicious," she began.

Her mother beamed. "You like it?"

"Wonderful, honey," said her father. "What's in here?"

"Lots of things," said her mother. Mrs. Fremont always said "lots of things" when she put something in that Mr. Fremont didn't like.

"It's delicious," Missy's father repeated, taking a third helping.

Missy saw her mother wink at her. "Mom, did you talk to Dad about my room yet?" she said.

"I noticed you didn't get very far on your clean-up project today," she answered.

Missy and Baby had stayed at the park longer than they'd expected. "But there's no place to put anything," said Missy. "I don't know where to start."

"There's a shovel out in the garage you can use," joked Mr. Fremont.

"Funny, Dad," said Missy.

Mr. Fremont put down his fork. "All kidding aside," he said, "we can't talk about redecorating your room until you show us that you're responsible enough to keep it clean."

"I know, but . . ."

"No buts," her father said flatly. "When you get rid of this stuff so we can see your room, Mom and I will let you redecorate it."

Missy stopped. "You will?" Her father nodded. Missy threw her arms around his neck. "Thank you, Dad. Thank you, Mom. Thank you, thank you, thank you!" Her parents laughed.

Missy stared soberly at them both. "I promise I'll get my room so clean, you won't even recognize it."

"Okay," said her mother. "We're counting on you!"

That night, as Missy lay in bed, she looked around her room. "How will I ever clean up this mess?" she wondered. She switched on the light. Next to her bed on the night stand sat a copy of *The Complete Decorator*. Missy thumbed through the magazine. There were so many great ideas. She already knew that she wanted a canopy bed and some hanging plants. An article called "Dressing Up Your Wall" caught her eye. Missy read the article carefully. It said that wall murals were one way of jazzing up a drab wall.

Missy looked around her room. "Maybe a mural would look nice on my wall," she thought. She wished she knew someone who could draw. Maybe her mother could help her. Mrs. Fremont was a kindergarten teacher, so she had to draw all the time.

Missy looked at the article again. "Organize a

painting party with your friends," the article suggested.

Missy suddenly sat up in bed. "Hey, wait a minute!" she said. "That's a great idea—a painting party with my friends. We could draw a mural of my life with Baby." Missy settled back on her pillow. That was it. She'd get all the girls in the class to help with the mural. And before they started, they could help clean her room. "What a brilliant idea!" Missy thought.

The next day in school Missy could hardly wait to propose her plan to her friends. During the first recess she gathered all her friends around her. "My parents just gave me permission to redecorate my room," she said.

"Neat," said Amy Flanders. "I want to be a decorator when I grow up. Maybe I can help."

Missy could see that her plan was working. "You can," she said carefully. "I'm going to be painting a wall mural of my life with Baby. Anyone who helps me clean up my room can paint part of the mural."

"Wow," said Emily Green. She was the best artist in class. "That sounds like fun. You can count me in!"

"And count me out!" said Stephanie Cook.

Missy took a deep breath. She'd forgotten about Stephanie. Ever since she'd moved here, her neighbor Stephanie had been giving her a hard time. Stephanie was the most popular girl in school. Missy's nickname for her was Ms. Perfect. "Everyone's invited," said Missy, ignoring Stephanie's comment.

"I always wanted to do a wall mural," said Wilhelmina "Willie" Wagnalls. "Remember Ms. DeLuca, the student teacher we had in school last year? She helped us do a mural—I think it's still hanging in Mrs. Shipman's room!"

"That's right," said Christine Coogan. "First we drew it on a sheet of graph paper and then we transferred it to the wall."

Missy was glad to learn this.

Stephanie folded her arms. "Wall murals are for babies," she said flatly.

"Waaah!" said Willie. She stuck her thumb in her mouth.

"Stephanie, you don't have to come," said Missy, trying not to laugh. "This Saturday is the clean-up party and next Saturday is the painting party."

Stephanie sniffed. "I wasn't planning to come! I have ballet on Saturdays. Besides, our whole house is about to be done by Maurice Chapereau."

"Who's he?" asked Missy.

Stephanie's eyebrows shot up. "You mean you don't know Maurice Chapereau—the world-famous designer?"

"Are designers the same as decorators?" asked Amy.

"Better, they're more expensive!" said Stephanie.

"That figures," said Willie.

"Wow," said Amy. "Maybe he can give us some advice."

Stephanie put her nose in the air. "Maurice

Chapereau doesn't do just *anybody's* house. He selects the ones he wants to work with." She eyed Missy up and down. "I doubt that he'd choose yours."

Missy stiffened.

"That wasn't very nice of you, Stephanie," Ashley Woods said boldly. Ashley usually stuck up for Stephanie.

Stephanie glanced around. "It's true," she said. "Why would he want to do Missy's dinky house?"

"What's so dinky about it?" said Missy. "I happen to like our house!" The knot of girls tightened around her.

"Just because you have a fancy decorator doesn't mean your house is going to look that great," said Willie.

"Yeah!" said Meredith Lilly. "You don't have to be snotty about it."

Stephanie tossed her long blond hair over her shoulder. "Humph," she said, staring at the group. "We'll see whose room turns out beautifully and whose looks really *atrocious*!"

Missy and the other girls stood silently for a moment. "We sure will." Missy grinned.

"Humph," said Stephanie for the second time. She turned on her heel and hurried off. Everyone watched her go.

Willie turned to Missy. "Can I paint the part when you first got Baby and he was just a tiny ball of fluff?" she asked. "I'm not too good at drawing dogs, but I think I can manage a fluff ball."

"Okay," said Missy. She looked around. "Who

wants to paint the time Baby went to camp with me?"

"I do," said Kate Heller.

"I'll help everyone with their drawings," Emily volunteered.

"We still have ten minutes of recess left. Let's start planning the mural now," said Amy.

"Good idea," said Missy. As she pulled out a piece of notebook paper and a pencil she noticed Stephanie standing in the far corner of the schoolyard, glaring at her. Missy waved, but Stephanie turned away.

"Oh, well." Missy shrugged. She picked up her pencil. "How should we start, you guys?" she asked her friends. For once in her life she wasn't going to let Stephanie Cook get to her.

That evening after dinner Missy was sitting at the kitchen table working on her math homework when she got a telephone call. "It's Willie," said the voice on the other end.

"Hi," said Missy. "What's up?"

"I just got my Girl Scout magazine today," said Willie. "You'll never guess what!"

"What?" said Missy. Sometimes Willie wasn't too specific.

"In an upcoming issue the magazine is doing an article on room redecoration. You'd be perfect."

"I don't get it," said Missy.

"They want to do an article about people who are redecorating their rooms," Willie explained. "You have to write them and tell them what you're planning to do. You also have to send a BEFORE picture. Then if you get chosen, they have someone come over and take pictures for the magazine."

"Wow," said Missy. "Do you really think they'd choose me?"

Willie laughed. "Are you kidding me? Once they see your BEFORE picture they'll be dying to see the AFTER effects! Here. Write this down."

Missy carefully recorded the information. "Thanks, Willie," she said. "I'll let you know what happens." Missy excitedly hung up the phone and looked underneath her kitchen table. Baby was curled up asleep. "Guess what, Baby," she said, nudging him with her foot. "We're going to be famous. What do you think of that?"

Baby opened one eye and wagged his stubby tail back and forth.

"That's what I thought," she said happily. She shoved aside her math book. "My homework can wait. Right now this letter to the magazine is more important!"

CHAPTER

2

"**D**ad, how does this sound?" said Missy. She and Baby stood next to the washing machine in the basement, where her father was practicing. He always practiced his viola down there. He said it was the quietest room in the house.

"Dear *Girl Scout Life*," Missy began. "Hi. My name is Melissa Fremont. I am twelve years old and my room needs redecorating. Here is what I plan to do. First, I am going to clean it up." Her father laughed. "What's so funny?" said Missy.

"Nothing," said her father. "Go on."

"Next, I am having a painting party with all my friends. We are going to paint a wall mural. It is going to be pictures of me and my Old English sheepdog, Baby. I am also going to have a canopy bed and hanging plants and a colorful rug. I hope you choose me for the magazine. I have never been in a magazine before. Sincerely, Melissa Fremont."

Missy's father applauded. "Bravo, bravo. Well said."

Missy was glad her father liked the letter. "Do you think you could take the BEFORE picture?" she asked. "Mom's busy." Besides teaching kindergarten, Missy's mother gave piano lessons after school and on Saturdays.

"Your mother's better with the camera," said her father.

"The film's already loaded. All you have to do is shoot," said Missy.

"Let's go, then," said her father. He carefully rested his viola on top of the dryer and followed Missy upstairs.

When Missy got to her room she dramatically swung open the door. "Ta-da!"

Her father looked inside and readjusted his glasses. "Is it my imagination or is this room getting worse?"

"I wanted my BEFORE picture to be really bad," said Missy. "I messed up the room even more."

"I'll say!" said her father. "This looks like a department store after a one-day sale."

Missy laughed and handed him the camera. "Could you take the picture with Baby and me sitting on the bed?"

"I don't see why not," he said. "Just clear a spot where I can stand."

Missy moved a few piles around and then called Baby over.

"Say Toscanini," said her father.

Missy gave the biggest smile she could. "Tos-ca-nini." The camera flashed. Seconds later the picture popped out of the bottom. "How's it look?" said Missy.

"You're missing part of your head," said her father. "Let's try one more time."

This time the picture came out perfect. Missy put it into an envelope with her letter and licked the envelope shut. "Wish me luck," she said.

"Good luck," said her father, grinning. "Now, if you don't mind clearing me another path out of here, I have to get back to Beethoven."

Missy spent the rest of the week getting ready for her cleaning party on Saturday. She bought two bags of chips, five large bottles of soda, some pretzels, and red licorice sticks. Ashley was going to bring her radio so they could listen to Rockin' Don on WROK-97.

Missy still hadn't told her mother about the cherry-soda stain on the carpet. She was waiting until after the room was clean.

Saturday finally arrived. The first person to show up was Amy. "Wow," she said when she saw Missy's room. "Your mom allows this much mess?"

"Only if I keep my door closed," said Missy with a laugh.

Amy surveyed the room. "Where are you going to put the mural?"

"Over here," said Missy. She kicked a pile of clothes out of the way and noticed the stain again. "I think I have to get a new carpet too."

"Hmmm," said Amy. "The rest of your carpet looks fine. Maybe you could cover that spot with a piece of furniture instead."

"Good idea," said Missy. "Maybe a new dresser or something."

Amy pulled a few decorating magazines out of her book bag. "I was looking through these for some new ideas," Amy said to Missy. "It says here that the way to dress up a room is with 'some attractive antiques.' "

Missy carefully studied the picture. She squinted her eyes and tried to imagine her room filled with antiques.

"Hi, you guys," said Willie, bursting into the room. Emily and Ashley were right behind her. "Wow. What a mess!" they all said at once.

Ashley sneezed. "How do you ever find anything in here?"

"I don't," said Missy. She grinned and tossed a large empty box toward Willie. "Catch."

Willie grabbed the box and tumbled to the floor. "What do you want us to do with these things?" she asked. Without waiting for an answer, she put the box over Ashley's head and knocked. "Anybody home?"

"Help," said Ashley. "I can't see."

"You're supposed to fill it up," said Missy.

"Oh, I get it," said Willie. She turned the box back over and climbed inside. "Okay, this one's done!"

Everyone started laughing, including Meredith, Christine, and Kate, all of whom had just walked in.

Willie tumbled back out of the box and solemnly pulled on an old Mickey Mouse hat that she'd found underneath the bed. "Listen to your captain," she said. "Work starts in exactly two seconds. Turn on the radio, Ashley."

"Right, Mickey," said Ashley. She blasted up the volume.

"Okay, guys," said Missy. "You heard the captain. Let's go!"

Soon all the girls were busy shoving things into boxes and singing along with Rockin' Don. Even Baby did some crooning while he helped load boxes.

"Do bob de bop, my baby," sang Willie and Christine at the top of their lungs. Willie had added a stocking cap on top of the Mickey Mouse hat and tied a turquoise feather boa around her arm.

"Missy, you still want this Candy Land game?" said Kate. "My little cousin wants one."

"You can have it," said Missy.

"What about this teddy bear?" asked Kate. She took the last licorice stick.

"I'm saving that for my own children," said Missy.

Everyone started laughing.

"What's so funny about that?" said Missy. "I have a dress that belonged to my great-grandmother." Missy's grandmother had given her the dress for a school project—a videotape of her family's history.

"Yeah, but that's a nice dress," said Ashley. "This is a *teddy bear*, for gosh sakes."

Missy rolled her eyes. "Oh, okay. Is it for your cousin?"

"No." Kate grinned. "Me. I always wanted a teddy bear." Everybody hooted with laughter.

With everyone helping, the room was clean in under an hour. It took another twenty minutes to stuff the filled boxes into the closet. "What an improvement," said Amy.

"Just don't show your mom the closet," Meredith advised.

When the room was finally vacuumed and the last bit of trash taken out, Willie collapsed on the bed. "Food," she groaned. "I need food."

"Open wide," said Meredith, dumping the last of the chips down Willie's throat.

For the rest of the morning the girls worked on how they were going to redecorate. They moved the bed to the other side of the room, put the old dresser in the corner, and decided where to put the hanging plants. With Emily's help they also decided what to put into the mural and actually did a first sketch on notebook paper. Everyone was excited when Missy told them about the letter she wrote to *Girl Scout Life*.

"If I get chosen," said Missy, "I'm going to make sure everyone gets to be in the picture!"

Willie held up the bottle of soda they'd all been passing around. "Here's to Missy," she said solemnly. "Hip, hip, hooray! Hip, hip, hooray! Hip, hip, hooray!"

Later, after everyone had left, Missy took her parents upstairs to show them the results. "Okay, you guys," she said when she reached her room. "Close your eyes."

She led them inside. "Open them."

"Wow!" said her father. "What a difference."

"I'd forgotten what a nice room this was," said her mother. She saw the spot on the carpet and frowned.

"Want to hear my decorating plans?" said Missy quickly. She explained about the canopy bed and the antiques.

Her mother glanced at her father. "That sounds lovely, Missy, but let's not forget the budget."

"What budget?"

"Antiques are very expensive," said her mother.

"They are?" said Missy.

"And canopy beds aren't exactly cheap," her father added.

"But I thought you were going to let me re-decorate however I wanted to," said Missy.

"Within reason," said her mother. She paused. "I saw an adorable white bedroom set on sale last week at L.S. Ayres. Would you like to go look at it?"

"Mom," wailed Missy. "Those things are for kids. I want to have a grown-up room."

Missy's parents looked at each other again. "Pat, what about Bundorfer's Antiques?" said her father. "I've heard their prices aren't bad." Missy saw her mother raise her eyebrows.

"Dad, maybe you could build the canopy bed," said Missy. "All we have to do is put up four posts and stretch some cloth across the top."

"Hmmm," said her father.

Missy turned to her mother. "I want to use the same cloth on the canopy as the curtains," she said. "It's called 'Poetry in Primrose.' Can you help me?"

Missy's mother didn't look thrilled. "Missy," she said, "this is a lot of work and you know what sort of a seamstress I am. Are you sure you don't want to stick with the bedroom set I saw at Ayres?"

Missy shook her head.

Her father cleared his throat. "Pat, if you can manage the curtains, I can manage the four-poster," he said. "How about it?"

Missy looked at her mother, who smiled.

"You're right," her mother said. "This is your room and you should be allowed to decide what you want. Just remember we're not the Rocke-fellers."

Missy threw her arms around her mother and grinned. "Thanks, Mom," she said. "My room is going to look so great, you won't believe it!"

Bundorfer's Antiques was located in an old house in downtown Indianapolis. Outside the house on a large porch were several stacked bureaus and dressers covered with an old sheet of plastic to protect them from the rain. As Missy and her father drove up, she could see a chained-up Doberman barking in the back yard.

Missy's father parked in front of the house. "Let's go have a look," he said.

They picked their way up the stairs and rang

the bell. The peephole slid open and shut and then a very old man who was no taller than Missy opened the door a tiny crack. "Yes?"

"Are you Mr. Bundorfer?" said Missy's father.

"Sometimes," said the man.

"We'd like to have a look at your antiques," said Mr. Fremont.

Mr. Bundorfer stared at Missy. "No children."

"She's not a child," said Mr. Fremont quickly. "She's a short adult."

Mr. Bundorfer gave a toothless grin and opened the door. "I like a fellow with a sense of humor," he said. "Come on in."

It took Missy's eyes a few minutes to adjust to the darkness of the room. Two cats disappeared under a sofa.

"Make yourself at home," said Mr. Bundorfer. "I'll be in the kitchen having my tea."

Missy watched Mr. Bundorfer shuffle away. She'd never seen so much junk in her life. "Dad," she whispered, "are you sure we came to the right place?"

"I sure hope so," he whispered back. "Charlie Higgenbottom in the oboe section told me this place has wonderful stuff." He cleaned off his glasses. "Let's just have a good look around before we do anything rash."

Missy nodded and headed off in the direction of the living room. Every room in the house seemed to be filled with furniture. There were lots of chairs without bottoms, tables missing legs, and saggy-looking dressers. In one corner was a stack of mirrors of various sizes. Missy wondered where Mr. Bundorfer slept.

She wandered onto a small enclosed porch off the living room. At first she didn't see anything that caught her eye, but then she noticed a very tall, dusty-looking piece of furniture. She climbed over a coffee table to get a better look.

The piece of furniture almost touched the ceiling, and it had two long doors on the front of it, like a cabinet. Missy tugged on the doors and they slowly creaked open. Inside were fifteen drawers each a different size from the others, perfect for holding all of Missy's things. And one of the doors had a mirror on it too.

"Dad, come here!" called Missy. "I think I found something I like!"

Missy's father and Mr. Bundorfer both appeared. "What's all the shouting?" said Mr. Bundorfer. "You're going to frighten the cats."

In her most polite voice Missy said, "Could you please tell me what this is?"

"A wardrobe," said Mr. Bundorfer. "What does it look like?"

Missy turned to her father. "Dad, this is just what I need," she said. "It'll hold all of my stuff and cover up the spot I made on the carpet."

Her father ran his finger along the outside of the door. There was at least an inch of dust. "Are you sure, honey? This is going to take up an awful lot of room."

Missy persisted. "I can get rid of that other dresser I've had since I was a baby," she said.

"The only other piece of furniture will be the canopy bed."

Her father turned to Mr. Bundorfer. "Sir, how much would you be willing to sell this for?" he said. He ran his finger along the dusty base again. "It needs a good cleaning."

Mr. Bundorfer cackled. "I'll practically give it to you," he said. "I didn't think I'd ever get rid of this thing. I fired the fellow who bought it."

Missy nodded her head up and down and crossed her fingers.

Mr. Fremont took one step back and squinted at the wardrobe again. "Okay," he finally said. "We'll take it."

"We will?" said Missy. She couldn't believe it.

"You do want it, don't you?" said her father.

"Yes," she said. "Yes, yes, yes, yes, yes!"

"Good," said her father. He turned once again to Mr. Bundorfer. "Okay, sir," he said. "What do you say we sit down for a moment and talk turkey?"

CHAPTER

3

The following Monday Missy couldn't wait to get to school and tell everyone about her weekend. Downstairs in the Fremonts' kitchen Missy's mother was busy stacking empty egg cartons on the counter. Her kindergarten class was going to use them to make jewelry boxes for the mothers.

"Morning, Mom," said Missy.

Her mother smiled. "You're awfully chipper today."

"I'm excited about my room," Missy said.

"When does your wardrobe get delivered?" asked Mrs. Fremont.

"Saturday," Missy answered. "Just in time for our painting party." She poured herself a bowl of cereal. "Do you think we could go to the fabric store today? I want to try and finish everything by Saturday."

"Hmmm. I have a student coming at three. Why don't we go after that?"

"Great!" said Missy. She finished her cereal and then looked around the room. "Where's Baby?"

"I think he's out in the garage with Dad looking through the scrap heap."

Missy excused herself and hurried to the garage.

"Hi, you guys," she called. Bent over the scrap heap were two rear ends, one furry and one regular.

Her father stood up and adjusted his glasses. "Just the person I wanted to see," he said. He held up the boards from her old lemonade stand. "What about these four posts?"

Missy paused. "The ones I saw in the magazine were round," she said. "Maybe we could try and find some like that."

"Okey-dokey," said her father cheerfully. "You're the decorator." He began searching through the pile again. "Here we go," he said. With a loud grunt he dragged a long piece of board out and swung it around. "How's that?"

"Perfect," said Missy.

Suddenly the woodpile that Missy's father was standing on shifted to the left. "Watch out, Dad!"

"Whoa!" shouted Mr. Fremont. As he stepped out of the way the board he was holding swung back around, knocking a can of pink paint off the shelf. Globs of "Pink Lemonade" started to ooze onto the pile of wood. "Quick! A rag!"

Missy grabbed an old T-shirt. "I've got it, Dad." She looked at her watch and gasped. "Oh, no! I'm going to miss the bus!" She threw down the rag and rushed out the garage door. "Sorry,

Dad!" The bus had already pulled up across the street.

"Hold it! Wait for me!" Missy yelled.

It was a close call. The bus driver, Mr. Covey, snapped the doors shut just as Missy made it inside.

"Sorry," Missy mumbled. She made her way to the back of the bus, where the older kids always sat.

"What took you so long?" said Stephanie. As usual, she was busy combing her hair.

"I was making plans for my new room," Missy puffed breathlessly. She took a seat next to Ashley. Across the aisle, Stephanie snickered.

"What's so funny about that?" said Missy.

"Yeah. What's so funny?" echoed Ashley.

"Nothing," said Stephanie, wiping the grin off her face. "I can't wait to see the results."

During lunch Missy told all the girls about her trip to Bundorfer's antique shop.

"You mean Bundorfer's *junk* shop," snorted Stephanie.

Missy just ignored her.

"My mom bought a few things at Bundorfer's," said Amy. "They looked beautiful, after she refinished them."

"Hey!" said Emily. "Maybe your mom could give Missy some tips!"

"Tips?" said Willie. She turned to Missy. "Hey, waitress!"

Missy grinned. "Cute, Willie."

Stephanie wrinkled her nose and mumbled something no one could hear.

"Did you hear from the Girl Scout magazine yet?" asked Willie.

"What Girl Scout magazine?" Stephanie interrupted.

Meredith patiently explained about the contest.

"How tacky," sniffed Stephanie. "A wall mural! *My* room is being done in chrome and leather. Maurice is going for depth."

A wicked smile crossed Willie's face. "Did you say Maurice is going *deaf*?" she said incredulously.

The other girls began to giggle.

Stephanie wasn't amused. "You heard me perfectly well, Wilhelmina Wagnalls," she said. She picked up her tray angrily. "Maurice happens to be the top decorator in the country. I think you all should try to take him more seriously." She walked off in a huff.

Willie shook her head. "That's too bad about Maurice," she said.

This time everyone burst out laughing.

When Missy got home from school, her mother was waiting for her in the kitchen. "Guess what?" she said. "You just had a phone call from *Girl Scout Life*. They want to photograph your room!"

Missy threw down her book bag. "You're kidding!"

"I'm not," said her mother with a laugh. "It must have been that BEFORE picture. They're coming on Saturday for your painting party."

Missy whooped with joy. "I'm going to be famous!" she shouted. She hugged her mother, she hugged Baby, she even hugged the chair. Then suddenly she stopped. "Oh, my gosh."

"What is it?" said her mother.

"There's so much to do. We have to make the bed, make the curtains, clean up the wardrobe." She stopped again. "Mom, what am I going to *wear*? I never even thought about that." She stared at Baby. "You're going to need a bath."

"Missy, relax," said her mother. "They want to see your room in progress, not finished. I think what they're most interested in is the mural."

Missy tried to remain calm. "Right," she said. "The mural." She hopped in the air again. "Mom, I don't believe it! They actually chose me!" She grabbed Baby's front paws and danced with him across the kitchen floor. "Baby, do you know what this means?" she said. "This means we're going to be famous!"

By the next day everyone at Hills Point School had heard about Missy's news. Even Missy's teacher, Ms. Van Sickel, made a big deal about it. She let Emily pass around the sketch of the mural and then had Missy explain what she'd done to get the magazine interested.

At lunch all the girls sat together and talked about what they were going to wear. Everyone, that is, except Stephanie. She sat by herself on the other side of the cafeteria, looking grumpy.

Missy stared at her. It bothered her that Stephanie was being such a pain. She picked up her tray and walked toward her.

"What do you want?" said Stephanie as Missy sat down beside her.

"I want to invite you to our painting party," said Missy.

Stephanie folded her arms. "No thanks. I'm busy."

Missy shrugged. "Okay," she said. "Have it your way."

The rest of the week sped by. On Wednesday night Missy helped her father sand the poles they were going to use for the bed. On Thursday she stayed up an hour past her bedtime, helping her mother cut the fabric for the curtains.

Saturday morning Missy woke up early. There was still lots to do. The fabric had to be fitted onto the frame, the curtains needed to be hung, and Baby had to have a bath. The girls were coming at ten and the photographer at twelve.

Missy tiptoed into her parents' bedroom. "Wake up, you guys," she said softly. "Rise and shine."

Her father rolled over and stared at her. He'd had a performance the night before and didn't get home until midnight. Missy gave him a big grin. "Hi, Dad. Time to get up."

"Coffee," he mumbled.

Missy's mother sat up and rubbed her eyes. "Missy! It's six-thirty!"

"I know," she said. "We've got to finish up before the magazine people get here."

Her mother yawned and then swung her legs onto the floor.

"Here's your slippers, Mom," said Missy. "The coffee's already on."

"Good girl," her mother mumbled. She covered Missy's father's face with a pillow. "Let's let him sleep a little longer," she whispered. "He had a late night."

Missy padded back down the hall. Maybe this would be a good time to give Baby his bath. "Here, Baby," she called. "Come out, come out, wherever you are." Baby wasn't too crazy about baths.

Missy started the tub and then looked some more. She finally found him squished against the wall under the kitchen table.

"I promised I wouldn't tell on him," said her mother. She was sliding the finished curtains onto the rods.

"Poor Baby," said Missy. She grabbed him firmly by the collar. "This'll take only a minute."

Willie was the first person to arrive. She was wearing one of her father's shirts. "That looks cute," said Missy.

"Thanks," said Willie. "Dad doesn't know I have it yet." Baby tumbled down the stairs and threw his paws on Willie's shoulders. "Wow. You look great!" said Willie. "I like your bow." She looked around. "So where is everybody else?"

"Not here yet," Missy answered. "Come upstairs. Dad needs help with the canopy."

Missy's father was kneeling on the floor, holding one of the poles. "Need help with your teepee?" said Willie.

Mr. Fremont grinned. "Just be good enough to hold this pole so I can bolt it onto the headboard, wise guy." With his free hand he groped under the bed.

"What'd you lose?" said Missy.

"My screwdriver."

"It's behind your ear!" chorused Willie and Missy gleefully.

Missy's father reached up. "I thought that ear felt a little heavy," he said. Missy laughed. Her father was always misplacing things.

It took a long time to put up the posts. "This is going to be nice," said Willie when they were finally finished. By now all the other girls had arrived and Emily was organizing the mural.

"Now for the fabric," said Missy proudly. She and her father had made a simple wooden frame, stretched the fabric across it, and stapled it on with a staple gun. All they had to do was set the frame on top of the poles.

"Careful," said Missy, lifting up the frame. She and Willie stood on the bed and gently lowered the frame onto the posts.

"It doesn't fit," said Willie. She hopped off the bed and stood back. "The poles are crooked."

Missy stared helplessly at her father.

"No problem," he said. He took out his hammer and banged one of the poles. "How's that?"

"Too far," said Willie.

"No, too close," said Emily.

"Maybe you should try bending the frame," said Amy.

"Missy, the men from Bundorfer's are here," called her mother.

Everyone rushed downstairs.

The wardrobe was lying on its side halfway inside the front door. It was even larger and dirtier than Missy had remembered.

"Wow," said Amy. "That's as big as a room!" The other girls nodded in agreement.

"Where do you want it?" said a big man smoking a cigar.

Missy pointed upstairs.

The other man, who was shorter and wider, picked up one end. "Let's go, Vinnie," he grunted.

The girls stood in a little cluster at the foot of the stairs and watched the men push and puff their way to the top.

"Go, go, go," whispered Willie. Meredith poked her.

"What do you think, Mom?" said Missy.

"It certainly looks as if it'll hold all your things," her mother answered.

"I bet there's even room for Baby in there!" said Christine.

Missy laughed and ran up the stairs. "I'm going to try to clean some of the crud off before the magazine people get here."

For the rest of the morning everyone worked. Mr. Fremont finally managed to get the poles straight, Missy got the first layer of dirt off the wardrobe, and Emily and the other girls mixed the paint and put down newspapers along the base of the wall. Now all they needed to do was transfer the mural to the wall.

Missy had just finished scrubbing the bottom drawer when the doorbell rang. "It's them! It's the Girl Scouts!" she shouted. Everyone began hopping up and down and screaming.

The door pushed open and in strolled Stephanie. She was wearing an expensive-looking new outfit.

"What are *you* doing here?" said Amy.

"Yeah!" said Willie. "You don't look like a Girl Scout to me."

Stephanie slowly surveyed the room.

"What do you want, Stephanie?" said Missy. She didn't like the way Stephanie had barged in.

Stephanie stopped, flung back her hair, and then arched her eyebrows. "I thought you all would be interested to learn that *Better Gardens and Homes* has just picked *our* home to be featured in the upcoming issue. They plan to photograph Maurice's work from start to finish."

Missy's chin dropped.

"The publicist and photographer are coming today to scout locations," Stephanie continued, "so I would appreciate it if you all would stay as far away as possible." She tilted her nose and turned to go.

No one said a word, but inside Missy was fuming.

Then suddenly Baby came bounding though the door, his tail wagging. Stephanie veered back. "Stay away from me," she warned. "I don't want dog hair on my outfit." She tried to step away.

"Watch out for the paint cans!" said Ashley.

Stephanie's foot came down on the floor, narrowly missing a container of red paint.

"Whew," said Meredith. "Close call."

"Get your horrible dog out of here," said Stephanie. "I mean it."

Baby lowered his head and growled.

"Help!" Stephanie screamed. "He's going to attack me!" She opened the wardrobe door and tried to climb inside.

"That's dirty . . ." Missy warned.

But it was too late. A huge blob of black crud came toppling down off the top of the wardrobe and landed on Stephanie's head. "Oooooh!" she screamed. "Disgusting! Get it off of me."

No one knew what to do.

"It's going to ruin my hair," Stephanie yelled, shaking her head. "I have to look nice for the magazine people." The blob was stuck in her hair.

"Help. It's about to disintegrate," Stephanie cried. "Get it off."

Missy winced.

"You all are hopeless," shouted Stephanie. She hurried stiffly across the room and then down the stairs, trying carefully not to jerk her head. Missy watched in amazement as Stephanie fled across the street.

CHAPTER

4

"**M**issy, what's all the noise in there?"

Missy looked over and saw her mother standing in the doorway. "Nothing, Mom."

Mrs. Fremont narrowed her eyes. "Was that Stephanie I heard?"

"It wasn't our fault, Mrs. Fremont," said Ashley, butting into the conversation. "Stephanie was getting out of Baby's way and she backed into the wardrobe. All this gunk fell on her." The other girls nodded in agreement.

Missy's mother sighed. "Maybe you should go over and apologize."

"But Mom, we didn't do anything."

Her mother gave her a look.

"Oh, okay," she said. "I'll go." She stared at her friends. "If the Girl Scout reporter comes, tell her to wait."

Missy grabbed Baby and hurried out the door.

"You're apologizing too," she said, dragging Baby across the street. "If it weren't for you, we wouldn't be in this mess." She rang the bell and tapped her foot impatiently.

When Stephanie opened the door and saw Baby, she jumped back in surprise. "*Now* what do you want?" she said.

"We're sorry about your hair," said Missy. She noticed the blob was gone. "Good thing that goop came out easily!"

Stephanie made a face. "No thanks to you." She gingerly leaned forward, still staying out of Baby's way. "Are you sure it's all out?"

Missy examined Ms. Perfect's scalp. "Yes, Stephanie," she sighed. Stephanie started to straighten up. "Hey, wait!" Missy said. "What are all those tiny white flakes?"

Stephanie gasped.

Missy grinned. "Just kidding."

Stephanie folded her arms. "Ha, ha. Very funny."

At that moment a car pulled into the Cooks' driveway. Stephanie broke into a big smile. "It's them!" she shouted excitedly. "The people from *Better Gardens and Homes*!" She gave Missy a little nudge. "You and your dog can go home now, Missy."

A large woman wearing wild sunglasses and bright red lipstick climbed out of the car. "Is this the Cook residence?" she asked. Without waiting for an answer she swept up the walk. "Andy," she shouted to a young man pulling camera equipment from the trunk, "make a note. Exte-

rior shot of the front door." Andy nodded and fumbled with his camera. The woman brushed past Missy, Stephanie, and Baby as if they weren't there. "Love the brickwood," she murmured.

Missy turned to watch the woman walk inside and felt Stephanie kick her shin. "Ow!" she cried.

"Beat it, you two," Stephanie hissed.

All of a sudden the woman turned around and lifted her sunglasses. "Hello, darling puppy," she purred to Baby. "Aren't you gorgeous!" Baby perked up and wagged his tail. The woman scratched Baby's ears with her long red finger-nails. "Andy, let's use him in the family-room shot, okay? Maybe with one of the kids." She stood up briskly and started to walk off.

Missy opened her mouth to say something, but before she had a chance Stephanie rushed past her, dragging Baby by the collar. "His name is Baby," Stephanie said with a big smile. "And I'm Stephanie. Stephanie *Cook*."

The woman stopped and looked at her. "Your dog is absolutely stunning," she said. "How long have you had him?"

"Five years," said Stephanie without even bat-ting an eye. "We just love him. He's part of the family." She leaned down and gave Baby a kiss.

Missy almost fainted.

Stephanie pulled Baby's collar. "Come on, Baby," she said. "Let's go to the family room and watch some TV."

Missy watched dumbfounded as Stephanie pushed Baby into the house. "Bye-bye, Missy," she said sweetly. "Nice of you to stop by and see us." Baby gave Missy a helpless look.

Missy grabbed Stephanie's arm. "Where do you think you're going with my dog?" she whispered under her breath.

Stephanie waited until everyone was out of earshot. "Don't be stupid, Missy," she said, still gripping Baby's collar. "This is Baby's big chance to be famous."

"But he's not your dog!" said Missy. Baby whined and strained at the collar.

"So what?" said Stephanie, jerking him back. She lowered her voice. "Didn't you hear the publicist say how gorgeous he looked? He might even make the cover!"

Missy winced. It was nice to know Baby would be famous, but still . . .

"Steffie, sweetie. What are you doing?" called Mrs. Cook. "The magazine people are here!"

"I've gotta go," said Stephanie. She patted Missy on the back. "Think about it."

"But what about my dog?" Missy repeated. "When do I get him back?"

"Oh, stop worrying about your stupid dog," Stephanie snapped. "I'll bring him back as soon as they leave."

"But I need him for the Girl Scout magazine," Missy protested.

"Where would you rather see him?" said Stephanie. "In some dinky Girl Scout magazine or in *Better Gardens and Homes*?" The door slammed shut.

Missy pressed her lips together and then hurried around to the back of the Cooks' house, where they had their glass-enclosed family room. Sure enough, Stephanie appeared a few seconds later. Missy hid behind a bush and watched as Stephanie draped herself across the sofa and then pushed Baby's rear end down so he'd sit at her feet.

Missy didn't know what to do. She didn't want Baby to miss what was happening at her house, but she did want him to have a chance to appear in *Better Gardens and Homes*. She looked at the clock in the Cooks' family room. It was nearly noon.

The publicist and photographer entered the family room. "Perfect!" she saw the publicist say. It looked as if they were rearranging Baby and Stephanie near the stereo.

Missy waited until the publicist had left the room and then she went up and tapped on the window. Baby rushed over.

"What do you want?" said Stephanie, looking completely irritated.

"Have they taken his picture yet?" said Missy.

Stephanie slid open the glass door. "Of course not," she said. "This is just a scouting trip. They aren't taking pictures until next week, when the house is finished."

"So give me back my dog," Missy said. "He's a prisoner in there."

"They haven't left yet," Stephanie said. "They may still decide to use us somewhere else. So far we're in only one picture." She flipped back a strand of hair. "By the way, the publicist said we look perfect together!"

Missy's eyes narrowed. How could Stephanie say that? Everyone had always told her that *she* and Baby looked perfect together. They even had the same curly hair that flopped down into their eyes.

The publicist walked back into the room. "Hi there." Stephanie waved. Missy felt herself being shoved out the door. The bolt clicked.

"Have you seen my bedroom yet?" she heard Stephanie say. "Maurice is doing fabulous things up there." Missy pressed her nose against the glass and watched Stephanie yank Baby toward the stairs. "Come on, Baby. Let's go show the lady our room."

Sadly, Missy headed home. She'd never had anything like this happen in her life. She wanted Baby to have his picture in the magazine, but at the same time it burned her up that Stephanie was getting her own way.

When Missy walked into her room, she had another surprise waiting. "What's *that* supposed to be?" she gasped, staring at the wall. The other girls had obviously been busy transferring the graph while she was next door.

"Do you like it?" said Willie from the top of the ladder.

"That doesn't look like Baby," Missy wailed. "That looks like a pregnant elephant."

"See? I told you!" said Willie. "I should never have been given this job."

"But you're the only one tall enough," said Emily.

Willie leaned over on the ladder and started to erase Baby's head. "Maybe I can fix it."

"Where's the reporter?" Missy asked.

"Not here yet," said Christine.

Willie dangled one leg through the ladder and started to hum. The ladder creaked and shook.

"Be careful," said Emily.

"It's coming off," shouted Willie. She waved her hands up and down. "Whee . . ."

The ladder tilted to the right.

"Stop kidding around," Missy said.

"It's not going to break," said Willie. She bent even farther. The ladder tilted onto three legs. "Uh-oh."

The next thing Missy saw was Willie being hurled through the air, her arms and legs swinging in all directions. "Help!" she yelled. Like a shot being fired out of a cannon, she flew across the room, landing squarely on top of Missy's new canopy. *R-r-r-rip,* went the fabric. Willie tore through the roof and fell with a plop into the middle of Missy's bed.

Everyone rushed over. "Are you okay?" said Missy.

Willie rubbed her leg. "I think so." She stared up at the piece of dangling fabric. "I'm really sorry, Missy."

Missy nodded numbly. She couldn't believe this was happening.

"Maybe we can fix it," said Amy. "Do you have any extra fabric left?"

Missy nodded a second time. She was afraid if she opened her mouth, she'd either burst out crying or kill Willie.

"Missy, phone," called her mother from downstairs.

Missy ran into her parents' bedroom, glad for an excuse to leave the room.

"Missy," said the voice on the phone, "this is Ellen O'Connor with *Girl Scout Life*."

"Yes?" said Missy in a hopeful voice.

"Missy, we're very sorry, but we're not going to be able to make it to your house today. The magazine has decided to hold off on the redecorating story for at least another six months."

Missy's heart sank. "But my room can't wait six months," she said. "We're redecorating it *now*."

"I know how much you've been looking forward to having us come," said Ms. O'Connor. "I'm really sorry to disappoint you."

A lump started in Missy's throat. "Will you still come in six months?"

"We'd like to, yes. Obviously your room will be finished by then, but we want to honor our commitment and run photos of all the rooms we'd previously chosen."

From where Missy stood, she could still see partially into her room. The girls had removed the canopy and were bent over the torn fabric. Behind them on the wall was Baby's half-erased head. "It's just as well," she sighed. "Things weren't working out too well today anyway."

After Missy hung up the phone she walked slowly back down the hall. "Who was that?" asked Emily.

"The Girl Scouts," said Missy. "They aren't coming."

"They're not?" said everyone at once.

Missy started to explain about the magazine, when Meredith interrupted. "Hey! What happened to Baby?"

"Yoo-hoo. Anybody home?" Stephanie burst through the door still hanging on to Baby's collar.

"Hi, Stephanie," said Missy glumly. Stephanie's timing couldn't have been more perfect.

Stephanie stared at the torn canopy, the filthy wardrobe, and the half-erased mural. "What happened in here?" she said.

"Nothing," said Missy. "We're working."

Stephanie ran her fingers over part of the mural. "Has your little Girl Scout reporter arrived yet?"

"They're not coming," said Ashley, opening her big mouth.

Stephanie smiled. "No wonder," she said. At that, she burst into shrieks of laughter.

"I don't see what's so funny," said Missy stiffly.

"Me either," said Emily. "We've been working very hard in here."

Stephanie pointed to the mural. "What's that? An elephant?"

Willie straightened up. "That happens to be Baby."

Stephanie laughed so hard she had to hold her sides. "I can't believe you're serious about this," she said, gasping for breath. "That's *Baby*?" She howled some more.

The group of girls glared at her. "I think you'd better leave," said Emily.

"Before somebody makes you," added Christine.

Stephanie headed for the door. "Don't worry," she said, still smirking. "I think I've seen enough for one day."

The girls quietly watched Stephanie disappear out the front door. "What a creep," Kate finally said.

"I wish we could get Maurice or the magazine people over here to judge for themselves," said Kate. "I bet they'd really like this room."

"Yeah!" said Meredith.

"What was Stephanie doing with Baby anyway?" said Willie.

Missy explained how Stephanie had pretended that Baby was her dog so that she'd get her picture taken.

"That's not fair!" declared Christine.

Amy nodded her head. "If anything, Baby should have his picture taken over here."

"But I *want* Baby to have his picture in *Better Gardens and Homes*," said Missy. "He'll be famous!"

Willie flopped down on the bed. "So why can't *Better Gardens and Homes* come over here and take Baby's picture? This room is as good as Stephanie's."

"Willie," said Missy, *"Better Gardens and Homes*

is a famous magazine. They don't just drop in if you ask them to."

"I know that," she said. "But if there were some way we could get them over here without their knowing it . . ." She smiled wickedly.

"Yeah!" said Kate. "I'd love to see Stephanie's face when they showed up here instead of there."

Missy's mind started to race. "Wait a minute, guys," she said. "I may have an idea. Stephanie said that the magazine is coming back to photograph her house next Saturday. Do you think we could have this room finished by then?"

"Sure!" they all chorused.

"Hmmm," said Missy with a thoughtful nod. "Then maybe there *is* a way to get the magazine people over. But first we have to play along with Stephanie and let Baby be photographed at the Cooks' house."

"Okay!" they all said eagerly. "What's the plan?"

Missy's voice dropped down to a whisper. It was a brilliant idea.

CHAPTER

5

Even with everyone's help, the room took a lot longer to finish than anyone thought it would. One of the biggest problems was the mural. Emily had tried to touch up Willie's art but had to leave before it was done.

That night when Missy's father got home from his performance, Missy brought him up to show him the room. "What are all those elephants doing?" he asked, pointing at the mural.

"I was afraid of that," Missy sighed.

She called Emily the first thing the next morning. "Can you come back and help today?" she asked.

At three o'clock the doorbell rang. It was Emily, holding a stack of books under her arm. Missy could see the title of the top one: *How to Draw Dogs.*

"I'm glad it's you," Missy said. "I tried to fix the mural again and now it looks even worse." She led Emily up the stairs.

"Hmmm," said Emily when she saw what Missy had done. She carefully opened her top book to the picture of the Old English sheepdog. Baby slunk into the room, looked up at the wall, and whined. Emily gave him a friendly pat. "Don't worry," she said. "Before I'm through you're going to look beautiful!"

Two nights later Missy and Amy were in Missy's room working on the wardrobe. It was finally starting to shape up with the help of Amy's furniture refinisher. "Now I know this stuff stinks," Amy said, pulling on a pair of rubber gloves, "but wait till you see the results."

Missy watched as Amy poured some of the liquid into an old pie tin and then dipped a pad of steel wool into it. Amy was so talented. She'd even fixed the canopy by covering the rip with some pretty lace that looked as if it belonged there.

Amy took the steel wool and started scrubbing a tiny area in one corner of the wardrobe.

"Wow!" said Missy. "Look at the difference!"

Amy nodded. "I told you."

Missy stared up at the wardrobe. "Do we have to do the whole thing like this?"

"Yep," said Amy, never breaking her rhythm. She jerked her head toward a paper bag next to her on the floor. "There's more gloves and steel wool in there."

Missy laughed. "Okay, okay. I get the message." She smeared some of the refinisher on the other door. The stuff was really slimy. "I wonder if Maurice Chapereau ever uses this."

Amy wrinkled her nose. "When you were at Stephanie's the other day, did you get to see what they'd done?"

"Not really," Missy said. "She wouldn't let me inside."

"She's going to *have* to let you inside next Saturday or our plan won't work. Right?"

"I know," Missy moaned. "That may be the hardest part of all."

Missy's mother stopped by her room. "Missy, I need to run to the store. Will you and Amy be all right by yourself for a few minutes?"

"Sure, Mom," said Missy.

Her mother stared at the wardrobe. "What a difference!"

"That's what I said." Missy laughed.

Ten minutes passed. Missy was concentrating on cleaning a large wood carving in the middle of the door that she hadn't noticed before. Outside the window she heard a loud thud.

"What was that?" said Amy.

Missy walked over to the window. "I don't see anything."

The two girls resumed their work.

This time the knock was unmistakable.

"Maybe it's a branch," Amy said, moving closer to Missy.

Missy cast a nervous glance into the hall. "Baby. Come here!" she called.

Baby trotted into the room.

By now the tree outside Missy's window was shaking violently. Baby flattened his ears and growled.

"Someone's definitely out there," said Missy.

"A burglar," Amy whispered. "Call the police!"

Missy paused. Something wasn't right. "Why would a burglar make so much noise?" she said. She crouched down and started creeping toward the window.

"Are you out of your mind?" Amy said.

"I bet you anything that's no burglar," said Missy. "I bet it's Stephanie Cook." She slowly pulled herself up and peeked over the edge of the windowsill. On a branch below, she saw a flash of blond hair. Missy slid back to the floor. "It's her all right," she said. "She's trying to spy on us." She wiggled over to the closet.

"What are you doing?" said Amy.

"You'll see," said Missy. Inside the closet, Missy dug through her boxes until she found what she wanted.

"A butterfly net?" said Amy.

Missy nodded. "Watch this." She stationed herself beneath the windowsill and motioned to Amy to hide behind the wardrobe. "Tell me when you see her," she said.

Outside the window, the branches shook even harder. Missy held Baby's mouth shut so he wouldn't bark and tried to concentrate on watching Amy.

Suddenly Amy's eyes widened. She pointed to the window and opened her mouth. "It's W—"

Missy leapt up. "Gotcha!" she roared, swooping down the net.

Willie let out a scream. "Help!"

Missy jumped back. "Willie! What are you doing out there?"

With her bright yellow hat, Willie looked like a giant canary caught in a bird cage.

"I tried to warn you," said Amy.

"I'm really sorry, Willie," said Missy, untangling her friend. "I saw the yellow hat and thought you were Stephanie."

"Didn't you hear me downstairs knocking for the last ten minutes?" said Willie, clambering into the room. "Since no one answered the door, I decided to take a short cut." She brushed off her shirt and glared at her friends.

Missy and Amy suddenly burst out laughing.

"What's so funny?" said Willie. "I came over to help you guys!"

"That was some short cut," said Missy, shaking her head.

"Yeah," said Amy, laughing even harder, "I thought you were a burglar!"

Now Willie started laughing too. "I see your point," she said. "Most people don't drop in through the window, do they?" She put the net back on her head and danced around the room. "Good thing it wasn't Stephanie," she said. "She'd probably still be screaming about her hair."

"Willie," Missy said, grinning, "just promise me one thing."

"What's that?" said Willie.

"Don't go out the way you came in," she said.

"Don't worry." Willie laughed. "Next time I'll leave the leaves right where they are."

By Saturday the mural was really starting to look the way Missy had hoped it would. Everyone showed up at Missy's house early, eager to finish their work.

"Hey, I have an idea," said Meredith, putting the finishing touches on Baby and Missy's lemonade stand. "Maybe I should put Stephanie in here, looking jealous." Missy and Stephanie had almost gone to war over the lemonade stand. Both had been competing to raise the most money for a class trip.

"I don't want to see her on this wall." Amy leaned in close, carefully painting the words CINCINNATI—200 MILES on a sign with an arrow. "But wait till she sees what we've done. *Then* she'll look jealous. Especially after her bragging all week long."

Missy's father dropped in. "Hey, I don't look so bad there," he said, pointing.

Missy frowned. "That's Susan, Dad. Remember, the counselor Cousin Tanya and I had at Girl Scout camp?"

Missy's father adjusted his glasses and leaned forward. "Oh, right."

"You're over there with your viola," Missy said.

"I drew you, Mr. Fremont," said Ashley. "Do you like it?"

Missy's father nodded. "Very nice, Ashley," he said. "I see you even included my big feet."

Ashley blushed. "That was an accident," she said. "I spilled some paint down there and had to make your feet bigger to cover the spot."

Baby came up and nuzzled Mr. Fremont's hand. "*You're* certainly well represented here," he said. He stared at the mural. "I don't think

I've ever seen quite so many versions of the same dog."

"It's supposed to be Missy's life with Baby," explained Christine. "That's why you see him doing so many different things."

Mr. Fremont smiled. "Ah," he said. "I see."

"Speaking of Baby," Missy interrupted, "it's time for him to have a b-a-t-h," she spelled.

"Again?" said her father. "He just had one last week."

Missy hadn't told her parents about Baby being photographed for *Better Gardens and Homes*. She wanted it to be a surprise when the photographer showed up at their house later. "I want him to look nice," Missy said quickly.

"But Missy," said her father. "Is that being a good hostess? Your friends are here today to help you finish the mural. Baby's bath can wait."

Missy waved her hand in the air. "It's okay, Dad. The girls don't mind, do you?" She shook her head from side to side so the girls would get the hint.

"No," they all chorused. "We don't mind."

Missy hurried past her father and started the tub. She'd waited until the last minute so Baby would look his very best. She even had a new bow for his hair.

"Baby, where are you?" she called. She dragged him upstairs from his hiding place behind the washing machine and with Willie's help lifted him into the tub. "You won't regret this," she said as she scrubbed away. "This is your big day."

Baby whimpered and tucked his tail between his legs.

"Okay. Final rinse," said Missy. She carefully got out every bit of soap and then fluffed Baby dry with a beach towel.

Afterward, she used the hair dryer to make his hair look just right. The bow was the finishing touch.

Missy sat down on the edge of the tub. "You look beautiful," she told him. "Wait until Stephanie sees how nice you are." She bent down and kissed his nose.

Baby's tail swished back and forth.

"Time to go," Missy said. She stopped by her bedroom, where the girls were just finishing up. "T minus two and counting," she told them. "Does everyone remember the secret signal?"

"We'll wait for you to get to the family room," said Emily. "Then when we see you scratch your ear, we go."

"Right," said Missy. "Wish me luck." With a determined expression on her face, she crossed the yard and walked confidently up Stephanie's front steps.

CHAPTER

6

Missy rang the doorbell. The door opened a tiny crack. "Who is it?" said Denise, Stephanie's little sister.

"Who do you think?" said Missy. "You only see me every single day at the bus stop."

Before Denise could answer, Stephanie rushed down the stairs and shoved her sister out of the way. "Mom wanted you upstairs, Denise."

Stephanie grabbed Baby's leash and pulled him into the hallway. Missy started to follow him inside.

"Oh, no, you don't," Stephanie said, pushing Missy back out the door. "Only Baby is invited." Baby looked at Stephanie and growled.

"But that's not fair," said Missy. "Baby and I go everywhere together." She noticed that Stephanie had on eye makeup.

"Not today you don't," said Stephanie.

Missy bit her lip. She had to stay with Stephanie and Baby or her plan wouldn't work.

Missy heard voices behind her and turned around. It was the people from *Better Gardens and Homes* pulling up in their car.

Stephanie grabbed Baby and pushed her way past Missy. "Hi, there," she waved to them. "Come on in."

Missy watched the publicist and photographer hop out of the car. A third person was also with them, a short woman with fuzzy brown hair. Since she was carrying a small notebook, Missy decided she must be the reporter.

While the publicist was helping the photographer unload his camera equipment, Stephanie was wasting no time. "I'm Stephanie Cook," she said to the reporter, "and this is my darling dog, Baby."

The woman shook Stephanie's hand. "Vicky Carlson. Features."

"And I'm Missy Fremont," Missy butted in. "I live next door, and I want to be a magazine reporter when I grow up."

Stephanie's eyebrows shot up.

"You do?" said Ms. Carlson.

"Yes," continued Missy bravely. "Ever since I was born. And when Stephanie told me you were coming today, I got so excited. I've always wanted to meet a real magazine reporter."

Ms. Carlson smiled. "No kidding?"

Missy nodded her head. "No kidding." She took a deep breath. "I was wondering," she said. "I've never seen a real reporter in action. Would it be okay if I followed you around for a while? I promise not to read over your shoulder or bother you."

Ms. Carlson paused. By now Missy could feel Stephanie shooting imaginary daggers into her back. "Sure. Why not?" Ms. Carlson suddenly said. "This is a good opportunity for you to see what reporters do."

"Oh, good," said Missy. Carefully avoiding Stephanie's gaze, she followed Ms. Carlson into the Cooks' front hallway.

Inside, the publicist and photographer were already setting up the camera lights. When Stephanie and Baby appeared at the front door, the publicist dropped what she was doing and rushed over. "How's my favorite poochie?" she said, giving Baby a kiss and completely ignoring Stephanie.

Stephanie's parents and Denise appeared and there were more introductions. That's when Mrs. Cook noticed Missy and Baby. "Stephanie," she said in a quiet voice. "I thought we talked about not having friends over today."

Stephanie nodded and smiled. "Right, Mom, but Baby's going to be in the picture with me, remember?"

"Oh, that's right," said Mrs. Cook. "You did tell me that, didn't you?"

"But *Missy* doesn't have to be here," said Stephanie, continuing on. "No one invited *her*."

"Yes, they did," said Missy quickly. "Ms. Carlson told me I could stay. I want to be a reporter when I grow up."

Mrs. Cook paused.

"Ask her," said Missy.

Mrs. Cook sighed. "Oh, never mind," she said. "Just try not to get in the way." She hurried back to be with her guests.

"Liar," hissed Stephanie.

"Look who's talking," Missy whispered back.

Mrs. Cook ushered everyone into the living room. "Maurice just phoned to say he's on his way," she told the group. "Would anyone care for a drink?"

"I would," said Denise.

Her mother gave her a dirty look. The doorbell rang again. "That must be Maurice," said Mrs. Cook.

"I'll get it, kitten," said Mr. Cook, rising from his chair. Stephanie's parents both looked like movie actors. Today Mr. Cook was wearing an ascot.

Ms. Carlson leapt out of her chair. "If you don't mind," she said, following him. The publicist and the photographer joined in.

Now only Missy, Baby, Denise, and Stephanie were left in the living room. Missy looked around for the first time. There were mirrors everywhere and hardly any furniture except for the long couch they were all sitting on. A strange-looking water fountain bubbled on the glass coffee table in front of them.

Missy leaned forward. "You should put goldfish in there," she told Stephanie.

"That's the stupidest thing I ever heard," Stephanie responded. "Don't you know a piece of sculpture when you see one? It's called 'Liquid

Locomotion,' and Maurice picked it out person-ally."

"I think we should fill it with grape juice," Denise giggled.

Stephanie stood up and pulled on Baby's leash. "Oh, puh-lease," she said. She yanked Baby toward the hall.

"Grrrr," said Baby. Without budging an inch, he casually leaned down and took a few noisy slurps from "Liquid Locomotion."

Stephanie gasped. "Stop that!" she said.

Drops of water dribbled off Baby's whiskers and onto the coffee table. He growled a second time and then took another drink.

Using all her strength, Stephanie tugged on the leash one more time. "You're coming with me," she said through her teeth. Baby shifted slightly to the left.

"Be careful!" said Missy. "You'll hurt him!"

"Are you kidding me?" said Stephanie. "Look at him." Baby was lying down on the carpet now, taking a little nap.

"Denise, Stephanie, come say hello to Maurice," called Mrs. Cook from the other room.

"Coming, Mommy," said Stephanie. She looked helplessly at Missy. "Do something."

"Oh, okay," said Missy. "Baby, come." Baby immediately leapt up and followed the girls into the other room.

Missy remembered Ms. Carlson and went to stand next to her. Ms. Carlson smiled and tilted her notebook a tiny bit so Missy could read it. She was interviewing Maurice Chapereau, a small

man wearing a purple leather tie with a matching beret.

"The marvelous thing about this project," Maurice was saying, "was that Nancy Cook gave me a free rein. It was as if I was starting with a blank canvas." He took a roll of fancy breath mints out of his pocket and popped one into his mouth. "Mint, anyone?" Only Denise took one. "Of course, that's a decorator's dream," he continued. Everyone murmured in agreement.

"Maurice darling, we'd like to set up our shots as soon as possible," said the publicist. "Why don't we start upstairs and work our way down?"

Maurice nodded. "Let's start with the master bedroom, shall we?" Missy noticed that Maurice had a tiny diamond in his right ear.

The little group trooped upstairs. The minute everyone got there, the publicist and photographer started moving some of the furniture around so they could get certain things they wanted into the picture. The publicist ran back to the car and returned with an armful of flowers. "What sort of vases do we have to work with?" she asked Mrs. Cook.

Maurice seemed a little nervous seeing everything get rearranged. "This is, of course, the master suite," he told Ms. Carlson as he popped another breath mint into his mouth. "My design objective in here was to reflect the contained simplicity which the room already manifested."

Ms. Carlson scribbled furiously. "Uh-huh. Go on."

Missy watched Stephanie choke up on Baby's

leash again. If she didn't stop it, Missy knew, Baby was going to get angry.

Stephanie's room was next. Just as she'd told Missy, it was all done in leather and chrome. Missy thought it looked like a doctor's office. "Where's your bed?" she asked.

"My lounge becomes a sleeper," sniffed Stephanie. "It's a way to utilize space."

Missy nodded. "What happened to all your stuffed animals?"

Stephanie dismissed her with her hand. "Gone." A few minutes later, when no one was looking, Stephanie whispered into Missy's ear. "Stop asking such stupid questions, dummy. Stuffed animals are for children."

"Okay, poochie," sang the publicist. "Picture time!"

Stephanie smiled and pulled up on Baby's leash. Baby growled. "Come on, Baby darling," she said. "Let's be a good doggie." Baby reluctantly followed her over to the sofa bed.

Maurice suddenly got very excited. "Where did the dog come from?" he said. "No one told me about the dog!"

"Doesn't he look gorgeous?" gushed the publicist. "Look how his hair enhances the tone of the room. Leather and fur. What an elegant statement!"

Maurice took another breath mint. "If I'd have known about the dog, I would have designed a room for him."

The publicist perched Stephanie on the arm

of the sofa bed. "Have poochie sit next to you," she said.

"Sit, Baby," said Stephanie.

Baby pretended to be deaf.

Using all her strength, Stephanie pushed Baby's rear end to the floor. "I said *sit*," she shouted. Baby stared helplessly at Missy again. Missy wished there were some way she could explain to him what was going on.

Stephanie slipped a tube of lip gloss out of her pocket and dabbed it on. She didn't even notice that Baby's bow was crooked.

"Look this way, please," said the photographer. "Smile."

Stephanie and Baby sat up for the camera. Despite the crooked bow, Baby looked gorgeous. Missy was glad she'd waited until the last minute to bathe him.

The photographer snapped away for a long time. He tried lots of poses and angles and even shot a few pictures without Baby and Stephanie. Finally he was finished. "What's next?" he said.

"My room," Denise piped up.

Missy glanced around nervously. Now that Baby was finished upstairs, she only had to wait until they got back down to the family room.

Stephanie choked up on Baby's leash again. "You behave," she told him sternly. Baby tucked his tail between his legs and looked unhappily at Missy.

Again Missy wished there were some way she could let Baby know that everything was going to be all right. Instead, she followed Ms. Carlson into the next room.

"This is *my* room," shouted Denise as if no one had ever seen it before.

Missy started to feel impatient. Everything was taking much longer than she'd expected, and following Ms. Carlson around was getting boring. Missy walked over to the window to see if she could spot Willie downstairs waiting for her signal. She strained her eyes.

"I bet you're confused by my reporter's shorthand," said Ms. Carlson.

Missy looked up at her. "What?" she said. Her thoughts were a mile away. Where was everyone? Willie was supposed to be in the bushes outside Stephanie's family room, and everyone else was supposed to be across the street.

Ms. Carlson tilted her notebook. "No wonder you're losing interest," she said. "I bet you can't read my notes, can you?"

Missy stared down at Ms. Carlson's notebook. "Uh . . ."

"It's important for a reporter to learn to record things quickly and accurately," Ms. Carlson continued. "To save time, I write 'hv' instead of 'have.' Or 'nt' instead of 'not.' " Missy nodded politely and glanced anxiously out the window again. Where *were* they?

Inside, the photographer picked up his light stand. "Vicky, we'll be in the family room," he said.

Missy panicked. The family room! She needed to be down there with Stephanie or their plan wouldn't work. The idea was to wait until Steph-anie and Baby were arranged on the couch. Then Missy was to give the signal to Willie, who was to open the Cooks' front door and pass the same signal on to Emily.

"We'll join you in a while," Ms. Carlson was saying. "I want to show Missy a few things first."

Missy wrung her hands and tried to think.

"Here's a list of common abbreviations," said Ms. Carlson.

Out of the corner of her eye Missy was re-lieved to see Willie sneaking across the street. At least one person was where she was supposed to be.

Missy shifted her position slightly so that Wil-lie could see her. She had to let Willie know she wasn't downstairs yet. Missy started furiously rub-bing the back of her head to try to get Willie's attention.

Ms. Carlson stared at her. "Are you all right?"

"Dandruff," said Missy quickly. "I've got it bad."

"Oh," said Ms. Carlson. She resumed her explanations.

Missy peeked out the window again. Willie was waving that she'd seen her. Now all Missy had to do was figure out a way to get to the family room.

Ms. Carlson finished her speech and Missy eagerly started for the door. "Let me tell you a little reporter's secret," said Ms. Carlson, pulling her back. She took a tiny tape recorder out of her pocketbook. "Always cover your bases," she said. "Listen." She attached a miniature ear plug to the recorder and stuck it in Missy's ear.

Missy could hear Ms. Carlson interviewing Maurice Chapereau.

"Just in case I lose my notes," explained Ms. Carlson, "I have a back-up."

Missy nodded politely and tugged impatiently on the ear plug. She had to get out of there. She glanced out the window again. Why was Willie giving her a thumbs-up sign? Missy suddenly gasped. Willie must have seen her pulling on the ear plug and thought she was giving the signal from upstairs instead of from the family room. "No! Wait!" she yelled, quickly pulling her hand away from her ear. "Willie, stop! I didn't mean it!"

CHAPTER

7

Missy watched in disbelief as Willie gave the signal to the other girls and then ran around to open the front door. Across the street Emily nodded and lifted a supersonic dog whistle to her lips. Although the whistle couldn't be heard by human beings, it always drove Baby crazy.

Missy crossed her fingers and hoped. Unless Stephanie had been holding on to Baby's leash when the whistle blew, their plan was ruined.

Seconds later Missy had her answer. From behind the house a brown and white streak flashed by.

"Stop. Stop this instant!" shouted Stephanie.

Missy couldn't believe it. Not only was the plan working, it was working beyond her wildest dreams. At some point Stephanie must have tied the leash around her wrist, and now that Baby was following the whistle, there was no way she was going to free herself.

Missy watched as Stephanie tried to dig her heels into the grass. Chunks of the Cooks' front lawn flew into the air. "Arrgh," tugged Stephanie. "Stop. You're going to pull my arm out of its socket."

Baby flattened his ears and kept going.

"Stephanie darling. Let go of the leash!" shouted Mrs. Cook, running behind her.

"I can't," Stephanie screamed. She waved her free arm in the air. "Listen to me, you stupid dog. Do what I tell you."

Missy grinned and clapped her hands together. "Come on, Ms. Carlson," she said. "I don't think you want to miss this!"

Missy ran downstairs.

"What's going on?" said the publicist, starting out the door.

"Follow me," said Missy, running in Stephanie's direction.

"I'm sorry I ever borrowed you, you awful dog," Stephanie was screaming. "What a mistake."

Baby veered to the right and took a short cut through the bushes. "Ouch! Slow down, will you?" said Stephanie.

Baby kept going until he screeched to a halt in front of Missy's house. Emily slipped him a dog biscuit.

"*You!*" said Stephanie when she saw all the girls assembled. "What are *you* doing here?"

"We heard the screaming and came out to see what was the matter," said Amy calmly.

"How's the shooting going?" asked Meredith.

Stephanie glared at the girls and tried to catch

her breath. Her blouse had come untucked and her right shoe was missing. Bits of leaves clung to her hair. "Sure, sure," she said, pulling a twig out of her mouth. She angrily untied Baby's leash. "You can take your stupid dog back, Missy."

The publicist stepped forward, looking very concerned. "Are you all right?" she said. "Your dog seems to have gone mad."

Stephanie's face turned red. "He isn't mine," she muttered.

"Stephanie!" said Mrs. Cook. "What have you been telling these people?"

"It's okay, Mrs. Cook," said Missy quickly. "I let Stephanie borrow him for the picture." She scratched Baby's ear so he'd wag his tail. "See? He likes having his picture taken!"

Willie gave Missy a nudge. Missy smiled innocently at the publicist. "If you think Baby is beautiful," she said, "you should see his pictures!" She pointed to her own bedroom window. "My friends and I have just finished painting a wall mural all about Baby's life." She paused politely. "Would you like to see it?"

The publicist looked at Maurice, who smirked. "I don't think so, darling," she said. "Not today."

"Why not?" interrupted Ms. Carlson. "It sounds interesting to me." She gave Missy a wink.

The publicist frowned and pulled Ms. Carlson aside. "Will you excuse us, please?"

For several minutes the two women whispered back and forth. The publicist kept shaking her head no and Ms. Carlson kept shaking her head yes. Now Maurice and the photographer butted in. Missy could see that the photographer was on Ms. Carlson's side and Maurice was on the publicist's side.

"Can't we do something?" Ashley whispered helplessly to Missy.

Stephanie slid over next to Missy. "Don't think I don't know what you're doing," she hissed under her breath. "It's never going to work, though. Maurice won't allow it."

Then Missy heard Ms. Carlson say something to Maurice about minding his own business or losing the story. Maurice's face got very red. Ms. Carlson returned to the group. "We'll be only a minute, Mrs. Cook," she said coolly to Stephanie's mother. "I hope you don't mind."

Mrs. Cook nodded. She didn't seem too pleased. Neither did Stephanie.

Triumphantly, Missy led everyone inside. "Mom, Dad, some people from *Better Gardens and Homes* are here," she called.

Missy's mother appeared instantly. "What?" she said. "You mean the magazine?"

Maurice Chapereau peered around the Fremonts' living room. "That's correct," he sniffed.

"They want to see my mural, Mom," explained Missy.

Her mother stared at the large group assembled in front of her. "Oh," she said in a flustered voice. "How nice. We've never had anyone from a magazine here before." She straightened a pile of sheet music on the piano. "Please make yourselves comfortable. I'll just go get my husband. I'm sure he'd love to meet you all." She rushed back out of the room.

Maurice gingerly sat down beside the publicist on the Fremonts' sofa. "Good grief," he groaned as he looked around. "Another early American living room. Ugh."

"You'd think people would be tired of it by now," the publicist replied.

Missy's friends were standing in a little knot by the door. "What are we waiting for?" said Amy.

Missy's mother swept back into the room. "I seem to have lost my husband." She moved a dirty coffee cup off the TV.

Maurice stood up. "That's all right, Mrs. Fremont. We're just here to see the little girl's painting." He extended a manicured hand to the publicist. "Shall we?"

"Oh. Right," said Missy's mother. "Go on up."

The cluster of girls eagerly moved toward the stairs.

Maurice's teeth glistened. "By the way," he said as he passed Missy's mother, "I absolutely love your early American decor, Mrs. Fremont."

"You do?" said Missy's mother.

Maurice nodded and turned to the publicist. "Don't you, Jessica?"

"Stunning," she said.

Missy's father suddenly appeared around the corner.

"There you are!" said Mrs. Fremont.

He was wearing a dirty T-shirt and some faded work pants. Missy thought he looked like Mr.

Wright, the school janitor. "Been doing some work in the garage," he announced. "What's all the hullaballoo?"

Missy grimaced.

Ms. Carlson stepped forward and stuck out her hand. "I'm Vicky Carlson," she said, smiling.

Missy's father stepped back. "Careful! I'm covered with engine grease!"

Missy rolled her eyes.

"Your daughter invited us in to see the mural she's been working on," said Ms. Carlson.

Missy's father wiped his hands on his pants. "Oh! No wonder she was so eager to fin—"

Missy stepped on his foot.

"I'm sure Missy can show you to her room," interrupted her mother. She turned to her husband. "These people are from *Better Gardens and Homes*, the magazine."

"Oh," said Mr. Fremont. Missy was sure her father had never heard of it.

"Say, Missy," her father said, "before you go upstairs, why don't I take everyone down to see that bookshelf I built in the basement?" He grinned at Ms. Carlson. "Carpentry's one of my hobbies, you know."

Missy's mother turned pale. The basement wasn't even unpacked from their move yet, and the bookshelf was falling apart.

"Really?" said Ms. Carlson. "We're going to be doing a story soon on home carpentry."

Maurice looked at his watch. "Vicky, do we have time for this?"

"Of course we do, Maurice," she said, gritting her teeth.

Missy saw her mother bolt down the basement steps. She was probably going to try to pick up some of the dirty laundry that was thrown all over the floor.

"Follow me," said Missy's father cheerfully. He led everyone toward the stairs.

Willie grabbed Missy's arm. "Your dad can blab forever," she whispered. "We may never get back."

"I know." Missy groaned.

The basement was dark and crowded. "I can't see," complained Ashley. "I have weak ankles, and I'm going to trip."

Missy's father turned on his work light. "Ta-da!" he said, shining it on the bookcase.

"*That's* what you brought us down here to see?" said the publicist.

"Don't you love it?" said Missy's father. "It's the first thing I ever built."

"Looks like it," Stephanie muttered.

Missy's father knelt down. "Let me show you how I put this thing together. First of all, I didn't spend a cent on lumber. It's all scraps. Can you believe it?"

Maurice snorted.

"Daaad," wailed Missy.

Her father looked up. "What, pumpkin?"

Missy's mother came to the rescue. "William, I think the girls are eager to show everyone the mural."

"I'll be only another minute," said Mr. Fremont. "I want Ms. Carlson to see these headless nails."

Missy sighed.

"William," said her mother in a firm voice. Baby barked and tugged on Mr. Fremont's pant leg.

"Maybe another time would be better," said Ms. Carlson diplomatically.

"Oh," he said. "Sorry." Everyone shuffled back up the stairs.

"Now what?" puffed the publicist when they reached the top. She stopped to catch her breath and glared at Ms. Carlson.

"Now we go to my room," said Missy, continuing up the next flight. "Follow me."

"This whole thing is a waste of time," grumbled Stephanie in Missy's ear. "As soon as Maurice sees your dumb room, he's going to burst out laughing."

Missy marched to her door and flung it open. "Do you like it?" she said to Maurice and Jessica, who were busy talking.

Maurice looked up with a bored expression on his face. "Oh, my goodness," he suddenly gasped. He pointed to the wardrobe, which was now a beautiful piece of cherry wood furniture. "Did you get that at Bundorfer's jun . . . I mean antique shop?"

Missy nodded.

With a delighted expression Maurice grabbed the publicist's arm and dragged her over to the wardrobe. "Jessica, look!" he said. "This was my first job. I bought this piece for old man Bun-

dorfer and then got fired because he hated it! I always said if only he'd clean it up . . ." He gazed rapturously at the wardrobe. "Wasn't I right?"

Everyone stared in amazement.

"Spectacular," Jessica agreed. She turned to Missy. "Who refinished this for you?"

"Amy and I did," said Missy proudly. The publicist looked impressed. So did Ms. Carlson.

Maurice spun around and took in the rest of the room. "This is fantastic," he said, flapping his arms in the air. "Nothing like the rest of the house. A completely unique ambiance. Using the canopy bed with the wardrobe was a fabulous idea."

"Thank you," said Missy modestly. Over in the other corner Stephanie's face was getting redder and redder.

Maurice darted over to the mural, where Baby was sitting patiently. *"Naif primitif,"* he said. "Brilliant! Who did you say drew this?"

"We all did," said Missy, "but Emily was in charge." She began explaining the pictures. "Here's when I got Baby; this is when we went to camp . . ."

Maurice was charmed. "What originality!" he said enthusiastically. "I love it!"

"Vicky darling," interrupted Jessica, "we *must* do something for the magazine, don't you think?"

Ms. Carlson winked at Missy again. "Absolutely." She opened her notebook and then motioned to the photographer. "How about a few pictures?"

Missy grinned. "I want all my friends to be included," she said. "After all, this was their idea as much as mine."

Stephanie stomped over. "You can't use Baby," she said. "He was in *my* picture first."

Baby whimpered and stuck his tail between his legs.

Jessica leaned down and puckered her lips. "Don't worry, poochie," she said. "You're so gorgeous that Auntie Jess is going to make an exception."

Stephanie stomped her foot on the floor. "But he *can't* be in both," she said. "That's not fair!"

The publicist narrowed her eyes.

"Never mind," Stephanie muttered. She folded her arms and stalked back to the other side of the room.

The photographer began arranging the girls around the mural. "Put me in front of my part," said Meredith.

"Me too," said Ashley. "I did Missy's father. See the guy with the big feet?"

"Let's make it look like everyone is busy painting," suggested the photographer. "Do you have a ladder?"

The girls groaned.

"No ladder." Missy laughed. "Not if Willie stays in the room."

"Ha-ha," said Willie. "Very funny."

The photographer arranged everyone in "natural poses" and then set up his camera. "Okay, ladies. Say cheese."

Missy waved her arms. "Hold it," she said. "I have a better idea. One, two, three, everyone say *Baby*!"

"*Baby!*" shouted the girls.

The flashbulb popped and the girls all cheered. Missy smiled happily to herself. It was going to be a great picture.